AM I BIG ENOUGH?

A Fun Little Book on Manners

OTHER BOOKS BY TIMOTHY YOUNG

Do Not Open the Box, 978-0-7643-5043-6
The Angry Little Puffin, 978-0-7643-4805-1
I Hate Picture Books, 978-0-7643-4387-2
Shadows on My Wall, 978-0-7643-4224-0
They're Coming!, 978-0-7643-4225-7

Copyright © 2016 by Julia Pinckney

Library of Congress Control Number: 2015948885

All rights reserved. No part of this work may be reproduced or used in any form or by any means—graphic, electronic, or mechanical, including photocopying or information storage and retrieval systems—without written permission from the publisher.

The scanning, uploading, and distribution of this book or any part thereof via the Internet or via any other means without the permission of the publisher is illegal and punishable by law. Please purchase only authorized editions and do not participate in or encourage the electronic piracy of copyrighted materials.
"Schiffer," "Schiffer Publishing, Ltd. & Design," and the "Design of pen and inkwell" are registered trademarks of Schiffer Publishing, Ltd.

Designed by Danielle D. Farmer
Cover design by Justin Watkinson
Type set in BocciText/Apple Casual/Huggable
ISBN: 978-0-7643-5053-5

Printed in China

Published by Schiffer Publishing, Ltd.
4880 Lower Valley Road
Atglen, PA 19310
Phone: (610) 593-1777; Fax: (610) 593-2002
E-mail: Info@schifferbooks.com

For our complete selection of fine books on this and related subjects, please visit our website at www.schifferbooks.com. You may also write for a free catalog.

This book may be purchased from the publisher. Please try your bookstore first.

We are always looking for people to write books on new and related subjects. If you have an idea for a book, please contact us at proposals@schifferbooks.com.

Schiffer Publishing's titles are available at special discounts for bulk purchases for sales promotions or premiums. Special editions, including personalized covers, corporate imprints, and excerpts can be creataed in large quantities for special needs. For more information, contact the publisher.

AM I BIG ENOUGH?

A Fun Little Book on Manners

Julia Pinckney

illustrated by Timothy Young

Schiffer Publishing Ltd
4880 Lower Valley Road • Atglen, PA 19310

I am Finn. I have a big sister and a little sister.

I see Daddy shaking hands with his friends.

AM I BIG ENOUGH
to shake hands with a grown-up?

I AM BIG ENOUGH!

Place your hand here to see if YOU are big enough!

I hear my big sister say **"please"** when she wants a cup of milk.

AM I BIG ENOUGH to say "please"?

Place your hand here to see if YOU are big enough!

I AM BIG ENOUGH!

I see Mommy wait her turn at the store.

AM I BIG ENOUGH
to wait my turn?

Sometimes there are two people and only one cookie.

AM I BIG ENOUGH
to share my cookie with my friend?

I AM BIG ENOUGH!

Place your hand here to see if YOU are big enough!

My sister helps Mommy with the baby.

AM I BIG ENOUGH
to help Mommy?

I AM BIG ENOUGH!

Place your hand here to see if YOU are big enough!

All the people at the library use a quiet voice.

AM I BIG ENOUGH
to use my quiet voice?

I AM BIG ENOUGH!

Place your hand here to see if YOU are big enough!

**Even though my hands are small,
I can do these things all, because . . .**

I AM BIG ENOUGH!

JULIA PINCKNEY

lives in Charleston, South Carolina, and is the proud mother of two sons with impeccable manners.

TIMOTHY YOUNG

has had a lot of fun jobs; he's been an animator, puppet maker, toy designer, sculptor, art director, illustrator, and graphic designer. He has designed for *Pee-Wee's Playhouse*, the *Muppets*, *Disney*, the *Simpsons*, and *Universal Studios*. Now he is the author/illustrator of six published picture books including *I Hate Picture Books!* and *The Angry Little Puffin*. He lives with his family on the Eastern Shore of Maryland.

Find out more about him and his books at www.creaturesandcharacters.com.